# Boris Starts School

D0495504

SOUTHWARK LIBRARIES

SK 1877988 3

For Dr Elizabeth Marsden - always a smile. C.W

For the amazing Early Years Team at Piddle Valley. Thanks for everything! T.W.

**OXFORD**
UNIVERSITY PRESS

Great Clarendon Street, Oxford OX2 6DP

Oxford University Press is a department of the University of Oxford.
It furthers the University's objective of excellence in research, scholarship,
and education by publishing worldwide in

Oxford  New York

Auckland  Cape Town  Dar es Salaam  Hong Kong  Karachi
Kuala Lumpur  Madrid  Melbourne  Mexico City  Nairobi
New Delhi  Shanghai  Taipei  Toronto

With offices in
Argentina  Austria  Brazil  Chile  Czech Republic  France  Greece
Guatemala  Hungary  Italy  Japan  Poland  Portugal  Singapore
South Korea  Switzerland  Thailand  Turkey  Ukraine  Vietnam

Text copyright © Carrie Weston 2007
Illustrations copyright © Tim Warnes 2007
The moral rights of the author and artist have been asserted

Database right Oxford University Press (maker)

First published in 2007 as *Oh, Boris!*
First published in this new edition in 2012

All rights reserved. No part of this publication may be reproduced,
stored in a retrieval system, or transmitted, in any form or by any means,
without the prior permission in writing of Oxford University Press,
or as expressly permitted by law, or under terms agreed with the appropriate
reprographics rights organization. Enquiries concerning reproduction
outside the scope of the above should be sent to the Rights Department,
Oxford University Press, at the address above.

You must not circulate this book in any other binding or cover
and you must impose this same condition on any acquirer

British Library Cataloguing in Publication Data available

ISBN: 978-0-19-275832-3 (paperback)

10 9 8 7 6 5 4 3 2 1

Printed in China

*With thanks to Michael Bond and HarperCollins for their kind permission
in allowing Paddington Bear to make three and a bit appearances in this book.*

Paper used in the production of this book is a natural, recyclable product
made from wood grown in sustainable forests. The manufacturing process
conforms to the environmental regulations of the country of origin.

| London Borough of Southwark | |
| --- | --- |
| SK 1877988  3 | |
| ASKEWS & HOLT | 29-Jun-2012 |
| JF | £5.99 |
| | |

# Carrie Weston • Tim Warnes
# Boris Starts School

OXFORD

UNIVERSITY PRESS

The day that Miss Cluck said there was going to be a new animal in the class, everyone was very excited.

When Miss Cluck said that the new animal was a **bear**, the other animals squealed with delight.

Leticia the rabbit wondered if it might be a fluffy pink bear, like the one on her lunchbox.

Maxwell the mole wanted a floppy brown bear with velvet paws.

The mice hoped for a bear in wellingtons and a duffle coat.

Fergus the fox cub thought any teddy bear would be just fine.

So, when the classroom
door opened. . .

and Miss Cluck
introduced Boris. . .

everyone. . .

# screamed!

For Boris wasn't a teddy bear.

He was an enormous, hairy, scary, grizzly bear!

Miss Cluck found Boris a seat next to Maxwell. Boris wanted to say 'hello' in his politest voice.

But as he sat down there was a loud **crack.**

It made Maxwell hide his face in his paws.

'Oh, Boris!' said Miss Cluck. 'We'd better find you a bigger chair.'

Miss Cluck gave Boris
a new book and a pencil.
He was very
proud indeed.

With a big, friendly grin Boris turned to show the mice.

But Boris
forgot how
**fierce**
his teeth
were.

He forgot how
**big**
his paws
were.

my new
friends

And he forgot how **sharp** his claws were.

Somehow, the mice got scattered
across the classroom.
Somehow, the pages of his new book got ripped.

 Somehow, there was panic everywhere.

'Boris is too **big!**' cried one little mouse.

'Boris is too **hairy!**' yelled another.

'Boris is too **scary!**'
they all squeaked together.

'**Oh, Boris!**' said Miss Cluck. 'Please
try to be more careful.'

At lunchtime everyone sat together.

There was not enough room on the bench
for Boris, but nobody moved up.

So he sat all by himself
and dipped his big paw
into the large jar of
honey his mummy
had packed
for him.

When lunch was over
Miss Cluck said everyone
could go off and play.

The mice began a game
of hide-and-seek.

'1 ... 2 ... 3 ...'

Everyone ran
to find a place
to hide.
But Boris
was too
big.

So Boris shut his eyes and counted instead.

'One... two... three...
**coming to get you,'**
Boris boomed.

'Eeek!'

'Stop! Stop!'

'No! No!'

Leticia shook
with fear and
clung to Fergus.

?

Maxwell ran
crying to
Miss Cluck.

'Let's go inside and play some quiet games,' said Miss Cluck, 'and Boris, please try to be less scary, dear.'

The animals sat together in a circle.

There was no space for Boris.

Boris had nobody to play with and nobody to talk to.
Tears filled his big, brown eyes. Large teardrops rolled
down his long nose and splashed to the floor.

'I'm a
hairy bear,'
he sobbed.

'I'm a
scary bear,'
he sniffed.

'I'm just a great
big
grizzly bear.'

It seemed like a very long afternoon.

At last it was time
to go home.

Miss Cluck stood and waved as the
animals set off through the woods.

Leticia hopped
along the bank.

Fergus chased
the little mice
round a tree.

Maxwell scampered
through the leaves.

Boris plodded along far behind.

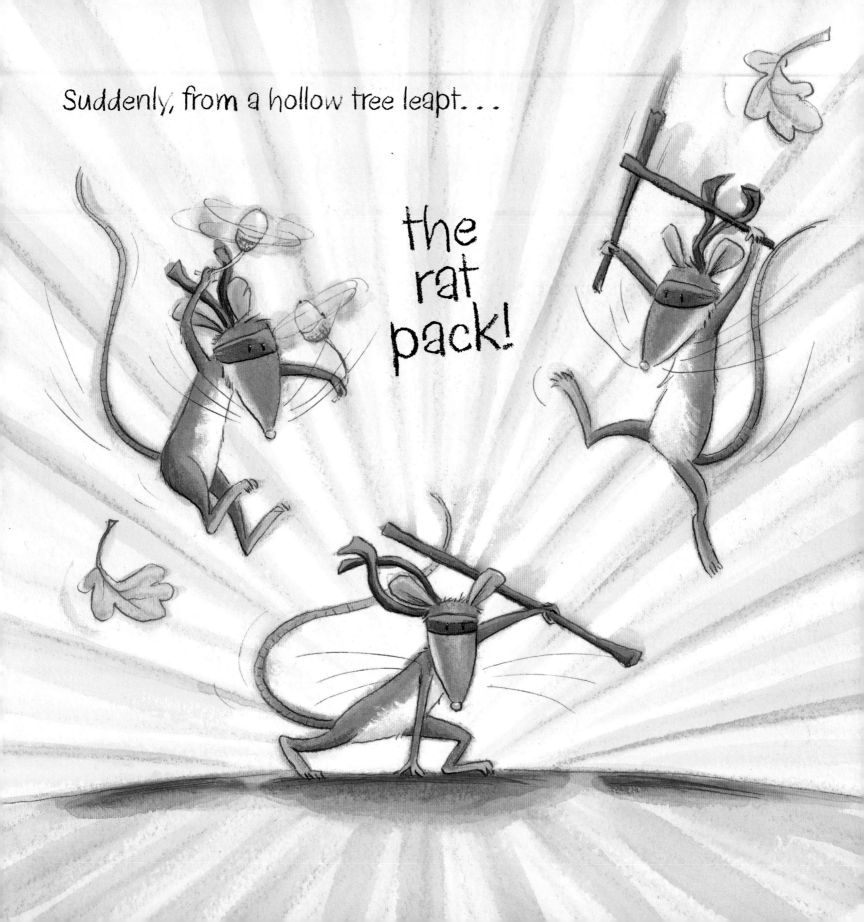

Suddenly, from a hollow tree leapt. . . .

the rat pack!

'Well, well, if it isn't the **boo-babies**,' said the meanest rat.

'Just look at the **scaredy-fox** and the **weedy** chicken-licken mice!'

poke!

'Help!'

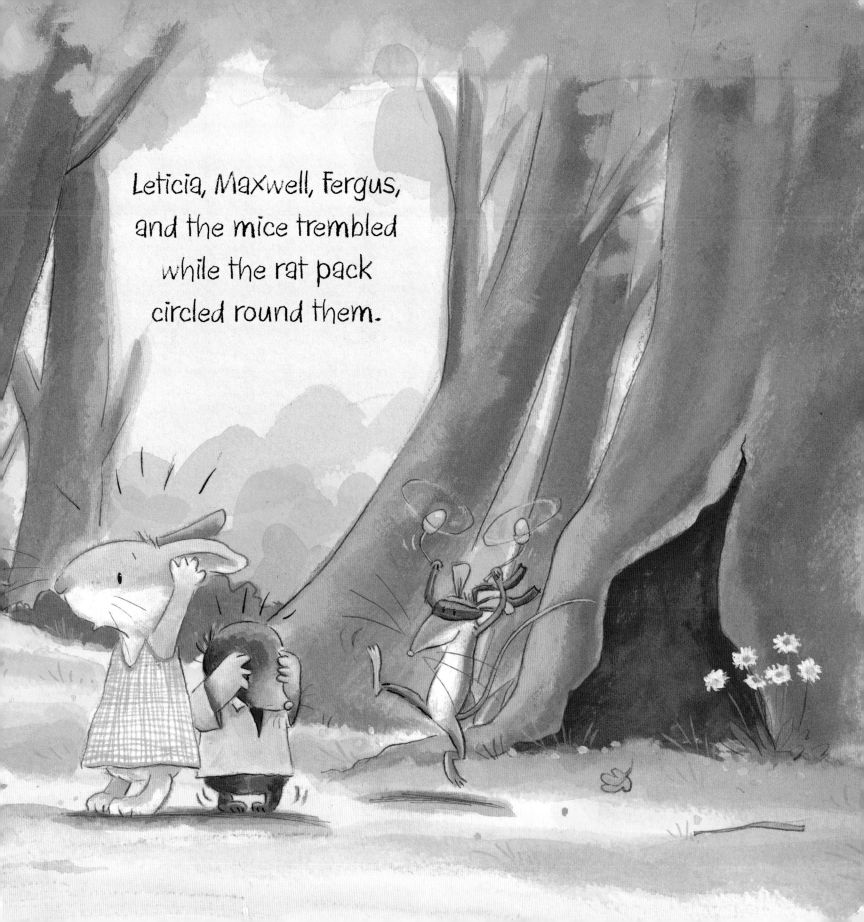

Leticia, Maxwell, Fergus, and the mice trembled while the rat pack circled round them.

The rats didn't see Boris
plodding along the path.

All Boris could see was lots
of excitement ahead.

He wanted to join the fun.

Huffing and puffing,
Boris stood up tall to greet
the new friends with
his **biggest**, widest
bear grin and. . .

'Quick! Run! It's a hairy, scary, grizzly bear!'

The rotten rats ran away as fast as their skinny legs could carry them.

'But I only wanted to say hello. . .' called Boris.

When Boris turned around,
the other animals cheered.

'Boris is a hairy bear,' they sang.

'Boris is a scary bear,' they chanted.

'We're so glad that
Boris is our grizzly bear!'

Suddenly, Boris felt very shy.
'If you're going to be a bear,'
he said very gently,
'then it's probably best to be a
hairy, scary, grizzly bear.'

The next day at school the animals couldn't wait to tell Miss Cluck how Boris had saved them from the nasty rat pack.

'Oh, Boris!' said Miss Cluck. 'What a good bear you are.'

At story time everyone rushed to gather around Miss Cluck. There wasn't much room once Boris had sat down.

But the rest of the class didn't mind one little bit. . .

they all had a soft,
warm place to sit, after all!